BAD PIGGIES

PIGGY ISLAND HEROES

Cody Smith

BAD PiGGiES

PIGGY ISLAND HEROES

— IT'S RAINING PIGS! —

INSIGHT KIDS

San Rafael, California

KING PIG

The leader of the pigs and the only pig who is allowed to eat eggs. His big secret is that he doesn't have any eggs in his treasure chamber.

PROFESSOR PIG

This brainy pig tries to help the other pigs with his contraptions, but unfortunately they are often turned into egg-hunting machines by Foreman Pig.

CHEF PIG

This intelligent pig is a cook and always plots to eat eggs himself and thus become King.

FOREMAN PIG

Foreman Pig supervises the building of all pigs' contraptions. He is very self-confident—and very incompetent.

MECHANIC PIG

Nosy little fixer.

SWEATY & SPOTTY

Eager but simple Minion Pigs.

THE RINGMASTER

Leader of the Piggy Circus.

PUMP

Dreams of becoming a star of the Piggy Circus.

KOFF & DUMPER

Beginners in mining.

STUMPY

Toughest miner in Pig City.

BIG SECRET

King Pig looked through his telescope at Professor Pig's lab for the fifth time that morning.

"He's acting so weird. What's he doing?" King Pig wondered.

He watched the Professor poke his head out of his lab window and sniff so hard that his snout could have fallen off. "What's that all about?" the King squealed. He peered through the eyepiece again. Now the Professor was on his roof and had hoisted something up a flag pole. His highness yelled,

"OH MY WORD!"

He twiddled the dial and refocused his telescope for a closer look. High on top of the pole something large flashed, spun around, then briefly came to a halt.

The King saw that it was a silver plate cut out to look like . . . the King!

He gasped and his tongue hung out at the sight of his shiny look-alike. He cried:

"SHINY! I WANT IT. I WANT SHINY!"

And what the King wants, the King gets!

Two cleaner Minions who were dusting and sweeping the Great Hall were startled by the King's cry. "Are you alright, your majesty?" they asked.

The King swung the telescope around and looked at them through the lens. "Who are you? You look so large!"

"We're Sweaty and Spotty. We work here," the Minions explained.

"Ah, of course I am!" the King said, confused.

The Minions gave each other a funny look.

King Pig took his eye from the telescope and stared in his weird way at the two pigs. "The Professor has got me," he hissed.

"Of course he has," said Sweaty, humoring the King.

"I'm on his roof, and I'm silver," the King babbled. "The Professor has always got big secrets, and I think he's using me for his next big secret!"

"You must be thrilled," said Spotty, still indulging him.

"No! No, I'm not! I want my big secret!"

The two pigs began to feel a little frightened and stepped backwards.

"Yes, Sire!"

"You don't understand," squealed the King. "I want his secret, and I want it now!"

Sweaty and Spotty, quite scared, froze on the spot.

"You two," said the King, "You will bring me the Professor's big secret!"

"We will?" Sweaty and Spotty asked.

"Why, yes," said King Pig. "And do it immediately!" He sent them off and followed them through his telescope.

Professor Pig sipped a cup of moss tea and took a break from building his weather vane. He looked at the sky, stuck his nose out of the window, and took a large whiff.

He noticed two pigs on a street corner staring in his direction and hollered,

"HELLO, THERE! CAN I HELP YOU?"

"Yes!" Sweaty called up at him. "Why do you sniff the air like that?"

"Oh, I'm checking for atmospheric precipitation," the Professor explained.

"Okay," said Spotty. "By the way, the King wants your big secret for himself."

He pointed toward the roof. The Professor looked up, puzzled.

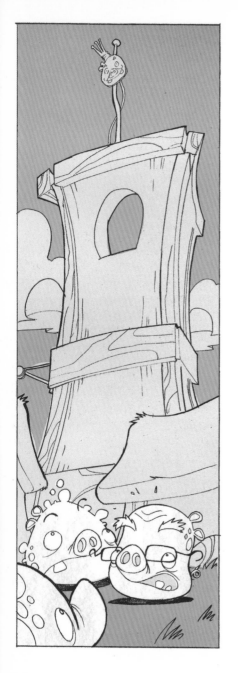

"He thinks that's my big secret? You mean my silver weather vane?"

"Yes!" said the Minions.

"Well, my experiment was a little secretive, I suppose. But that to which you refer, well, I'm afraid I need to keep hold of it for now. Its absence could affect the results of my test."

The Minions didn't have a clue what he was talking about.

The Professor saw their confusion and said, "I'm afraid the King can't have it. . . ."

With that, Spotty and Sweaty turned and left.

"He's a funny guy, don't ya think?" asked Sweaty.

"A bit nuts if you ask me," said Spotty.

The Professor cried,

"WHAT I MEANT TO SAY IS THAT HE CAN'T HAVE IT . . . JUST YET!"

But they were already gone. "What odd little fellows," he mumbled.

Back at the castle, the King was beside himself with the news.

"HE SAID NO?"

Pacing about, he bit his lip and said, "We shall sneak out under cover, and I'll have my big secret tonight!"

Sweaty said, "But Sire, there's a storm a-comin'!"

The King looked out of the window. "Nonsense! It's clear outside."

"It is now," agreed Sweaty, "but when a storm's a-comin', my 'ed swells and my snout runs like a river." Right on cue, his head swelled to twice its normal size and goo dripped from his snout. Sweaty grinned, pleased with himself.

"Wait a minute," said Spotty. "You said 'we.'"

"Yes!" sputtered the King.

"THIS TIME I'LL MAKE SURE YOU DO THE JOB RIGHT!"

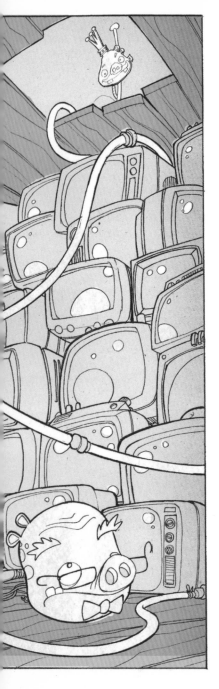

Professor Pig's weather vane spun wildly in the gathering storm. Inside his home, monitors and televisions were piled high to the ceiling, only a small part of the weird and bizarre stuff he collected. He didn't understand any of it but always tried to use it for his experiments.

The weather vane pole had pierced the roof and the monitors. The Professor exclaimed,

"OH, FIDDLESTICKS! I'VE PUT A HOLE IN MY ROOF!"

Outside, lightning flashed and thunder shook the lab.

"I think I'll have another cup of moss tea and fix it later," he thought.

Outside, the King and his duo trudged through the raging storm.

Sweaty's head was so swollen that he was floating like a balloon, going higher and higher.

"I've never been this big before," said Sweaty. Spotty had stuck a sink plug in his friend's nostril and was holding on to him with a chain. Sweaty bobbed wildly in the wind.

"You . . . ! Melon Head!" the King shouted to Sweaty. "Get up there and grab that big secret!"

The wind blew so strong that Spotty could hardly hold on to Sweaty. To keep Sweaty from floating away, he tied the chain around the King's body.

Thunder roared and lightning crackled. The Professor peered through the window, and in the rain, three shadowy figures were lit up by a flash of lightning.

"Good grief," he said. "What are they doing?"

"Grab it with your teeth!" Spotty shouted to his pal.

King Pig squealed, "Shiny thingy, shiny secret thingy!"

Sweaty swung back and forth. His jaws snapped, but he missed the target by a pig's whisker. Then, with a gigantic effort, he firmly clamped his chompers over the tin head.

"Yesss!" he shouted triumphantly through clenched teeth.

Then it happened!

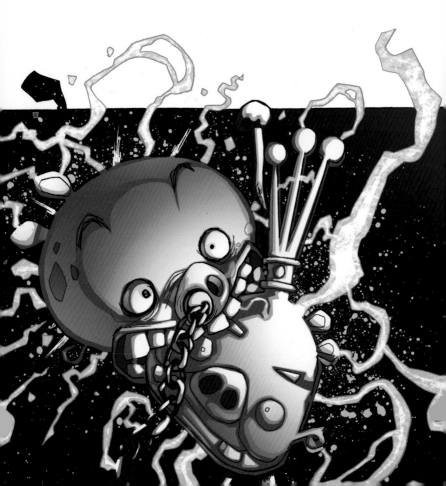

A giant bolt of lightning hit the pole and rattled through Sweaty's teeth, down the chain, and into the King! They both twitched, shook, sizzled, and sparked. They glowed like fireflies and smelled of fried smoky bacon!

Spotty had let go and was spared the shocking experience. Enjoying the display, he exclaimed,

"COOL!"

The lightning then shot straight down into Professor Pig's lab. Electricity surged through the monitors, sparking them to life. The room filled with deafening sounds and hundreds of images flashed across every screen.

The Professor watched in wonder as snapshots of cars, volcanoes, spaceships, advertisements for baked beans, and strange cities filled with light and color flickered before his eyes. None of it made sense to him!

It lasted just a few short seconds, and then the screens went black and silent. He gasped,

"HOW . . . EXTRAORDINARY!"

The storm passed.

The Professor went to bed with a cup of steaming moss tea. He was exhausted but his head was filled with ideas.

King Pig sat in a puddle of water. He stank of smoky bacon and whimpered in disappointment. He'd watched his big secret disappear in a zap of lightning and a puff of smoke.

Sweaty was back on the ground. He'd shrunk and was much smaller than normal. He was a changed pig! He smiled at his friend with his new, glossy chompers, courtesy of the lightning bolt.

Spotty admired his friend's new look. "C-O-O-L," he purred.

"YOU LOOK GREAT!"

King Pig looked up from his puddle and saw Sweaty's teeth. "Ooh, are those your secret teeth?" he squawked.

"I WANT THEM! SHINY TEETH!"

"Let him get his own," Sweaty said to Spotty, and they left the King alone in the rain and mud without his big secret.

THE HAUNTED MINES

Dumper and Koff had just qualified as miners. Their new helmets showed that they could work in the Earwax Mines deep below Hog's Head Mountain. There they would dig for the square rocks used in Piggy Contraptions and the soft green stone that would be sculpted into magnificent figures of Piggy history.

At the graduation, the band played a celebratory tune to send the graduates on their way.

BLOOMP-AH! TOOMPAH! TOOT-TOOT!

Dumper and Koff had always wanted to be miners, and now that they finally had their hats, they couldn't wait to get started!

The band played their last note and dashed off to band practice. They piled into an old, rickety vehicle, sped down the road, and almost ran over Dumper and Koff in their hurry. Koff shouted,

"ROAD HOGS!"

A huge, tough-looking hog called Stumpy was put in charge of Koff and Dumper on their first day. He had the reputation of being the toughest miner in Pig City.

When they arrived at the mines, they lit their candles, sat in the mine-shaft lift, and made the long descent into the abyss of the "inner ear."

At the bottom of the shaft, a mine car took them even deeper.

Koff loved ghost stories and on the way down he told the tale of the Phantom Miner. "Pigs say his spirit haunts the mine . . ." Koff said, spooking even himself.

"Hey, zip it with that nonsense!" growled Stumpy. "They're just dumb stories to scare piglets."

"Grumpy Stumpy," murmured Koff to himself.

At the end of the tunnel they got out and walked into the stale, chilly gloom.

"Why is it so cold?" shivered Dumper.

"This is the deepest tunnel," Stumpy said. "But I'll have you warmed up in no time."

Koff licked his lips and asked, "Oh, have you got any soup?"

Stumpy pressed his face into Koff's and shouted,

"NO! NOW, PIGS, DIG!"

His loud voice echoed around the tunnel, and a puff of dust fell from the ceiling.

"Careful! You'll bring the roof in," said Dumper.

Grumpy Stumpy growled,

"ZIP IT AND DIG!"

Dumper and Koff chipped carefully at the green rock while Stumpy worked like a machine.

Later, Koff paused and whispered, "Dumper! Did you hear that?"

Dumper heard nothing at first. Then, it came . . . a long, ghostly wail that traveled out of the darkness.

W-E-E-A-A-W-O-O-O!
R-A-A-R!

"What is that?" squeaked Dumper.

"It's nothing!" barked Stumpy, even though he looked nervous. "It's probably . . . air pockets!"

"B-B-But . . ." stammered Koff.

"I said, dig!" Stumpy shouted. His voice echoed and bounced around the cavern.

A deep rumble shook the walls, loosening dust and bits of rock. And then . . .

C-R-R-A-C-CK!

A huge crack appeared, and a ton of rubble crashed down around them. The dust eventually settled to reveal the disaster.

"Stumpy, look what you've done!" Dumper said, coughing.

"Me? Don't blame me! It must have been the air pockets," Stumpy stammered.

"It was the Phantom!" howled Koff.

Stumpy's eyes widened with fear.

"We're trapped!" wailed Koff. "We're doomed!"

"Be quiet," scolded Dumper. "We need to find another way out."

"We're doomed!" cried Koff. The tunnel shook menacingly again.

"Be quiet," hissed Dumper and Stumpy.

M-M-W-A-A-R-R!

"Gotta go," squealed Stumpy, who ran into the tunnel as fast as he could.

Dumper looked at Koff in disbelief. "He left us!" they gasped.

K-E-E-A-W-O-O-O!

Another scream split the air, and the two ran after Stumpy.

Eventually, it was silent again, and the three pigs searched for an exit.

"Do you know where you're going?" Dumper asked Stumpy. "I'm sure I've seen this rock before." Stumpy just huffed.

Lit by the pigs' candle headlamps, flecks of gold sparkled on the tunnel walls and congealed into thick seams. The tunnel widened and became a cave of gold! The place glittered and gleamed in the light.

"Ooh, nice," cooed Koff.

"It's worthless!" huffed Stumpy.

Koff said, "I've heard that any pig who eats it will go mad!"

"You must eat it every day then," sneered Stumpy.

Koff spotted two tunnels at the back of the cave. "Hey look! Which way now, guys?"

For ten minutes, Dumper and Stumpy argued about which tunnel to take, but couldn't come to an agreement. Eventually they decided to flip Koff like a coin. They'd take the left tunnel if he landed on his head, and the right one if he landed on his tail.

Unfortunately, Koff landed on his side, so they let him choose. Koff chose left, and Stumpy complained the whole way.

Soon the howling returned, louder and scarier than ever.

V-O-O-O-O-O-O-R-A-A-W-O-O!

"Whoa," cried Stumpy, who ran down the tunnel white with fear.

"He moves quickly for a big fella," said Koff.

When they caught up with him, he was a quivering mess.

"I wish you wouldn't keep running away like that," said Dumper.

"Oh no!" said Koff. "I think we're in trouble."

They were standing on a narrow stone bridge across the center of a deep, yawning chasm.

Far below them, an oozing river of bubbling emerald slime slid along like a green snake.

"Blimey!" said Koff. "That was close! We might've fallen off the edge."

Suddenly and without warning, the bridge crumbled under Koff, and the poor pig fell screaming into the green doom below. Where poor Koff had just been, there was now a gaping hole.

"Oh no! Poor Koff," Dumper whimpered and turned to Stumpy, but he had run away. Dumper ran over the bridge as fast as he could.

Y-E-E-O-O!!

The dreadful howls went on and on, sending chills down his spine. He found Stumpy, who was a bigger gibbering wreck than ever!

"What'll we do now?" Stumpy cried out.

"Let's stay cool and carry on," said Dumper, trying to calm down the big pig.

Then the spooky wails stopped!

Dumper's candle sputtered and spat, then went out. Then Stumpy's flame blinked a few times and died. Unable to even see their own snouts, they felt their way forward.

Stumpy screamed,

"UGH!"

"Something touched me!"

"I think that was me," said Dumper. He didn't dare say it but thought to himself, "He's a bit of a baby for such a tough guy."

They were alone, in the pitch-black darkness and clammy silence.

Suddenly, a pale blue glow appeared ahead of them. It looked like daylight.

"Look! I found a way out," boasted Stumpy.

They squeezed through a narrow opening and entered a gigantic cave.

Huge, perfectly formed blue crystals jutted out of the ground. There were clumps of luminous foxfire mushrooms and pools of water with small glowing fish.

Dumper groaned, "You didn't find us a way out, but congratulations, you did find us another cave."

Stumpy looked into one of the pools, and all of a sudden, a glowing fish leapt clear out of the water and tugged at his beard. He screamed,

"YAAARGH!"

and ran around like a crazy pig until he collided face-first with the biggest crystal in the cave and knocked himself out cold.

"What is his problem?" sighed Dumper. He grabbed Stumpy by the beard and dragged him out of the cave.

Eventually Dumper managed to find the way out. Everything was enveloped in wonderful daylight.

Stumpy stirred. "What's going on?" he croaked.

Above them, a waterfall cascaded over the rocks. The forest canopy stretched out below. They recognized the place: It was the top of Hog's Head Mountain.

The weird noises began again, but this time, they sounded different.

B-L-APITY-BARP!
R-ATIPOOP-I-DOOP!

"The band sounds quite good!" said a voice behind them. "They must come here to practice."

Dumper jumped around to see . . . "Koff!" he cried.

"You're alive!" cheered Dumper.

"'Course I am, silly," said Koff casually. "That green lava was weird stuff. It was like . . . a thick, carpety, moving moss! It dropped me off nearby, actually."

Koff carried on, "And I've solved the mystery of the noises, too!"

Dumper and Stumpy looked over the edge and saw the band playing their instruments in the shelter of the Mouth Pool. The noise reverberated around the rocks. The racket must have traveled through potholes and gaps to echo in the mines!

"Well, I knew it was the band all the time, of course," Stumpy lied.

"Whatever you say," said Koff generously.

"I suppose this racket led us out of there," said Dumper. "We better go down and thank them!"

Later, Dumper and Koff walked back home in the fresh air to tell their friends about their crazy day.

Stumpy stayed behind and spoke to the band. He was sick of being the hardest and toughest miner. "It was all an act," he confessed. "What I really need," he said, "is a complete change." So, he joined the band and discovered his new talent: playing the triangle!

TING!

THE KING'S EGGS

King Pig's birthday was just days away, and for his birthday he demanded two things: lots of presents and a banquet even bigger and better than last year's.

The King demanded: "I want eggs! Eggs are what I want!"

Foreman Pig took care of the presents. He made all of the Minions in Pig City donate a gift. Then, on the big day, he planned to tell the King that all of the presents were from him!

Chef Pig was always annoyed that Foreman was the first to finish his birthday tasks.

"It's so unfair," Chef complained.

"Look, you've already got all the presents!"

"Yes I have, haven't I?" gloated Foreman Pig, admiring a huge tower of gifts piled high in the Royal Present Room.

Chef got stressed out every year, and Foreman always teased him about it.

"There's not much time until the big day, is there?" Foreman said. "Do you need any help?"

"No thank you! I'll manage quite well," Chef sulked, faking confidence.

Foreman chuckled, "Well, I'm going to relax while you squirm," and off he swaggered.

The King always wanted his dream food on his birthday, but eggs were impossible to find at the best of times. So every year, Chef had to invent crafty alternatives to put on the table.

Whenever the King took a bite, he always noticed the substitute.

Last year, Chef gave him shaved coconuts. The year before that, he tried white balloons, but they all popped. Three years ago, Chef gave him melons painted white, but the greedy King tried to swallow them whole and nearly choked. It was a disaster!

Every year was tougher than the last, but now Chef was out of ideas.

He stared out his window and wondered,

"WHAT AM I GOING TO DO? I'M ALL DRIED UP!"

If he didn't give the King what he wanted, he'd be in big trouble.

Outside, Chef saw two Minions driving by in a buggy. He had an idea and called them over. After Sweaty and Spotty introduced themselves, Chef smiled insincerely.

"I have a very special mission for you both," he said. "You're going to make the King's birthday the best ever!" He continued, "You must search Piggy Island and bring back anything that looks like an egg. "Anything!" Chef added, "By the way, if you do get a real egg, put it aside for me so that I can . . . check it for quality." His mustache quivered, and one eye twitched.

If Chef got hold of an egg, he could kick the King off the throne and become ruler.

His twitching made Spotty and Sweaty nervous.

"I'd help out, but I've got a bad back," Chef lied. He had no intention of helping. He gave them a stern look, and added,

"BUT FAIL, AND IT'S THE DUNGEONS FOR YOU BOTH!"

Sweaty reassured him, "Hey! We're the hogs for the job, Chef!"

As they left, Spotty gave Chef some advice, "You should rest that back of yours."

"Yes, perhaps I should," murmured Chef. He then celebrated his genius by going to bed.

Spotty and Sweaty bounced around in their buggy and trailer as they drove off road into the Square Forest. Swarms of buzzing mosquitoes descended on the pigs.

"This is no fun," winced Spotty. The maddening bloodsuckers made him itch like crazy. Sweaty, however, casually licked them off himself and then feasted on Spotty's swarm.

"Yum," he purred. "Crunchy and tasty."

Spotty exclaimed, "Stop eating and drive faster! Let's get out of here before I'm eaten alive!"

Together they roared off into the pines at full speed.

Sweaty found an egg-shaped pinecone and popped it in his mouth.

"No! Keep it for the King," Spotty said, and Sweaty spat it into the trailer.

"Spoilsport! I was hungry," he moaned.

"You're always hungry!" Spotty said.

In a cottonwood they found a delicate, large, egg-shaped cotton ball amongst the mass of fluffy white blossoms. Sweaty stuck his tongue out and snagged it on one of the sharp thorns.

"Ow!" he yelped.

"Blimey, Sweaty, do you ever stop eating?" asked Spotty. They carefully plucked the cotton ball and put it in the trailer.

"Eggcellent," they said and built a fire to keep themselves warm as they slept.

The next day they found a huge termite mound.

Sweaty's tummy rumbled. "Grub time," he said.

They dug into the nest and dined on the squirming, juicy mass. Later, under the shade of a tree and with a full belly, Spotty burped. "I couldn't eat another termite," he sighed, and they dozed off.

When they awoke from their siesta, they found a massive egg half hidden in the dirt.

They didn't see that it was made of thousands of tiny termite eggs stuck together.

"Eggcellent-ay!" they said, and put it in the trailer with the rest of their loot.

Back in Pig City, Chef awoke from the best two days of sleep that he had ever had. For a second, he thought about the Minions. Then, he smacked his lips lazily and went back to sleep to dream about his greatest banquet being enjoyed by a very happy King Pig!

By mid-morning, the Minions reached Moorlands. It was a frightening, foggy place. Strange, tiny lights danced about in the mist. The pigs recalled the legends of will-o'-the-wisps that guided careless pigs to a squelching boggy doom.

Ignoring the lights, they moved on.

Later, Spotty found a huge, yellow, egg-shaped mushroom in the gloom.

"SHELL WE?"

he joked and placed it in the trailer.

Back in Pig City, Chef was very stressed.

"WHERE ARE THOSE MINIONS, FOR GOODNESS SAKE?"

His mustache twitched more than ever as he looked for them for the hundredth time. Still, they were nowhere in sight.

The Minions headed home, driving around the base of the Crown Mountains.

The snow was deep and hard. Icy winds blasted them numb.

Sweaty found a fantastic egg-shaped rock.

"I'm not sure this'll get past Chef's beady eyes," said Spotty, so he covered it with snow. "Hey! I think I've cracked it," he cheered.

"That's brilliant!" said Sweaty, impressed with the bigger, whiter 'egg.'

The King's birthday finally arrived.

He had already received his presents from Foreman Pig.

It was time for the banquet, and he was so excited!

Chef, however, was a bag of nerves. The table was bare. There was no sign of his scouts, and therefore no grub for the party.

"What a lovely banquet you've put together," Foreman Pig whispered to Chef.

The King screamed, "I'VE GOT MY PRESENTS, NOW WHERE'S MY FOOD? I'M STARVING!"

Suddenly, the great doors of the hall flung open.

"Here it is!" Sweaty and Spotty cried out triumphantly. Tired and proud, they waved the bags of food over their heads.

Chef dashed over, grabbed the bags, and slammed the doors in the faces of the stunned pigs left outside.

"Yes! Yes! Here it is, Sire!" Chef declared and spilled the bag's contents onto the huge banquet table.

The King stared in disappointment at the small meal.

"Is that it?" he screamed at the pathetic collection.

"Ah, but," Chef stammered, "don't be fooled by the size of the feast, your majesty. This . . . this will be a royal treat!"

The King looked unconvinced.

"That's right!" Chef carried on, "This will be a feast you'll never forget!"

Then things got worse for Chef.

The King got a tickle in his snout.

A-ACHOO!

He sneezed and blew the delicate cotton egg to dust. The next egg started to quiver and shake as if alive. Chef gasped in horror as thousands of squirming termites hatched and ate the mushroom egg and pinecone in seconds.

Foreman Pig couldn't stop himself from laughing at Chef's bad luck.

The King looked at the last egg and panicked.

"I'll have that!" he said and stuffed the snowy egg into his mouth. He took a big bite.

CRUNCH!

His teeth cracked on the icy stone. The monarch howled, "Ooww! Chef! You idiot! Your egg broke my lovely teeth!"

"To the dungeon with him!" the King screamed.

"For how long, Sire?" Foreman smirked.

"Six months, no . . . a year!" the King squealed.

Poor Chef paled. Foreman chuckled as he locked the cell door.

Shortly thereafter the King placed Foreman Pig on cooking duty, but his food was terrible.

Foreman eventually ended up in the dungeon for a week due to his offensive cooking, and Chef was released so that he could once again feed the King properly.

Sweaty and Spotty were happy to accept a new mission for His (toothless) Majesty: to find him a dentist!

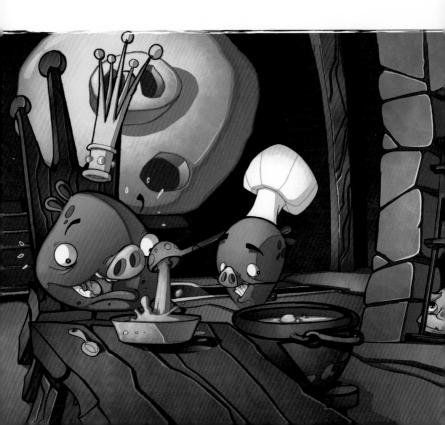

GARDEN IN GLOOM

Chef's kitchen garden usually reaped a rich and diverse harvest, but not this year. He desperately needed help, as his garden had no crops and the King might be forced to eat grass. The King hated grass!

Chef called on Mechanic Pig, even though he grated on Chef's nerves. After all, he was smart and good at fixing things.

"My garden's sick!" complained Chef. "Everything is wilting."

"Chef, you've done the right thing by calling me in," Mechanic said in his annoying, precise tone.

"I'm sure I can 'unearth' the problem in no time." Mechanic turned his blue cap to the side and snorted at his own joke.

"JUST LOOK AT THIS PLACE!"

Chef grumbled. "There's no bumper crop of Tongue Fungus or Bellybuns, and hardly a Snout-Hair Shoot in sight!"

Chef groaned, "I've even tried using a new water supply, but that doesn't seem to help."

"Hmmm," said Mechanic. "Just show me around and leave it to me."

Chef showed him a patch of dry ground with a bit of wood sticking out of it.

Mechanic pointed to the lump of wood and asked, "What's this?"

"It's supposed to be Skin Scrape. I use it for sauces in my recipes."

"It's a stump," blurted Mechanic.

"Excuse me, but that 'stump' is usually covered with lovely, smelly, purply, oozing fungus," Chef squeaked.

!!GROSS WARNING!!

SKIN SCRAPE

1

Rub a pig's back on the stump. Skin flakes fall to the base of the stump.

2

Place some sweaty hogs' heads against the stump. Sweat drips down the stump.

3

Weird-looking mushrooms will grow!

"And just look at these Snout-Hair Shoots!" He pointed to a few wispy, yellow sprigs poking out of some gravel underneath a Purple-Poople tree. "My nose hair always grows a better crop than this pathetic show!"

Mechanic took a peek up Chef's nostrils.

"Maybe these days your nostril hair is past its expiration date," he rudely suggested.

Chef snorted at Mechanic, "I have the highest grade nostril tuft, thank you very much!"

!!GROSS WARNING!!

SNOUT-HAIR SHOOTS

① Pluck a pig's nostril hairs.

② Plant them in the ground.

③ Weird -looking stems with toothy petals will grow!

Mechanic studied the dry land. Something moved in the grass, and a crab scuttled past him. He screamed,

"WHAT THE HECK!"

Chef stared in surprise at the crab. "How odd," he remarked.

Mechanic asked, "Where does your water supply come from?"

"You were too busy, so I asked another pig to make me an endless supply of water," replied Chef.

"Hmm," murmured Mechanic.

"He seemed to know what to do," said Chef.

"Hmm," Mechanic said again and sniffed the soil, licked it, then made a funny face.

"What're you doing?" asked Chef.

"I'm gathering evidence," Mechanic said.

Chef thought, "What a funny way to do it!"

"Do you know much about hogriculture?" he asked.
Mechanic Pig boasted, "I know more than most."

"Hmm," thought Chef, "what a know-it-all!"

Mechanic looked down his snout at Chef Pig. "Perhaps
you're a better chef than a gardener?" he said in a superior
tone.

Chef sulked, "Well, Foreman Pig said I'm a very good
gardener."

This annoyed Mr. Know-It-All. Mechanic didn't like
Foreman Pig. He had the impression that Foreman was a
very dim, jealous, and troublemaking hog.

Mechanic Pig turned to leave, "Well, go and ask him for
help! Go and get a poorly qualified pig!" He huffed, "I've got
other jobs to do!"

Chef sputtered and backtracked. He really needed Mechanic's help. "Well, what does Foreman know, anyway? Maybe I am a little rusty in the garden these days." Chef didn't like to beg, but he saw that more groveling was needed. "I'm sure you're the hog for the job!" He flattered Mechanic Pig some more, "You're so skilled!"

It worked. Mechanic loved being called skilled. He huffed and turned around.

"See this blue cap?" asked Mechanic.

"IT'S AN EXPERT'S CAP! SO, LISTEN TO THE EXPERT AND LET ME DO MY JOB!"

Chef looked at the blue hat and thought, "It's just a cap . . . but it sits on a big head!"

The "expert" carefully surveyed the garden.

"That's dune grass," he observed.

Chef replied, "I never noticed it before. Is it normally found this far from the seashore?"

Mechanic just made more notes and looked at the sad collection of Tongue Fungus and Booger Balls.

"Hmm," he murmured to himself. "These Booger Balls are very poor, very poor indeed!" He pointed to the wrinkled specimens. "How big should they be?"

"Usually as big as your head," said Chef cheekily.

BOOGER BALLS

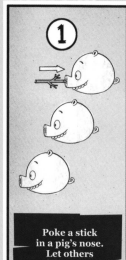

①
Poke a stick in a pig's nose. Let others have a go.

②
The stick becomes heavy.

③
It "ripens" or snaps with the weight of too many boogers.

TONGUE FUNGUS

①
Chop a square tree down. Cut a plank of wood from it. Feed pigs strong cheese.

②
Let the pigs lick the wood with their slimy, cheesy tongues and sneeze on it.

③
Mushrooms will grow on the plank!

They walked deep into the garden. "Watch out!" Chef called out. "You almost flattened my Bellybuns!"

Mechanic looked down. "What? This? They look terrible!"

"But why?" wailed Chef.

"It has to be the salty earth!" remarked Mechanic.

"Salty earth?" repeated Chef. His mustache twitched. The ground was dusty and cracked, with patches of flaky brown moss.

!!GROSSEST OF GROSS WARNING!!

BELLYBUNS

① Peel a strip of tree bark and lay it on the ground, rough side up.

② Make a pig rub his bottom over it. Shake dead beetles on top and sneeze on it. Repeat.

③ Large, hairy, blue-green nuts will have swollen and ripened!

"Hmm," Mechanic murmured. "This soil is really dry. You said a pig came and fitted a new water supply?" he said suspiciously.

"Well, maybe it's not working properly," said Chef.

Mechanic studied the dry garden. The castle cast a long shadow in the afternoon sun, and beyond it, Pig City spread out in every direction. He shouted,

"THIS DOESN'T ADD UP!"

Mechanic smelled a rat. "Well, this water supply isn't working, is it? Show me what he did!" he demanded.

"Must I?" asked Chef.

"You must," insisted Mechanic.

Chef reluctantly led him up the garden path to a huge bush at the foot of the castle. A large pipe poked through the greenery. It dripped water, making a large pool. It was the first sign of moisture Mechanic had seen in the garden. He peered into the water and couldn't believe his eyes.

"Hmm," he squinted.

"What?" asked Chef tensely.

Mechanic said, "There are crabs in here, and look, sea urchins, seaweed, and even an octopus!"

"That's nice," said Chef nervously.

"But we're a long way from the sea," Mechanic added. Chef bit his lip, unsure how to reply.

"Hello, and what's this?" asked Mechanic as he pointed out long orange hairs stuck to the pipe's opening. Chef went pale.

Mechanic exclaimed,

"ALL BECOMES CLEAR!"

Chef looked around. "What a lovely day it is!" He knew he was in trouble.

Mechanic looked stern and cleared his throat as if he were about to give a speech.

"Is this the mustache hair of Foreman Pig?"

"Well . . . " Chef gulped and fidgeted, ". . . maybe."

Mechanic continued, "Did you happen to hire Foreman Pig to create an endless supply of water for your garden?"

Mechanic's hard stare made Chef sweat. "Yes, well, you were busy . . . and I needed help. I thought he was good," he confessed.

Mechanic studied his notes. Dry salty soil, poor crops, the crab, for goodness sake! "It all makes sense," he said.

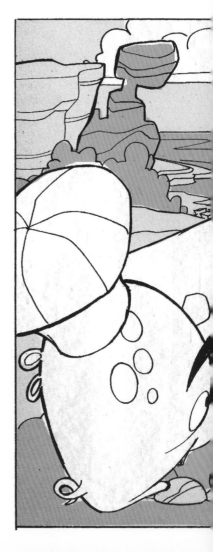

"The orange hair was a dead giveaway!" Mechanic's face was so smug he could have won first prize in a smug competition!

"Pardon me?" said Chef.

"Your clever little friend rigged you up an endless supply of water, all right," declared Mechanic.

He parted the bush to show Chef the pathway of the water pipe that stretched and wound its way down the Royal Road, past the harbor, and straight into the ocean.

"Congratulations. You may not have much of a garden, but you have a lovely beach!"

An endless supply of water indeed. "Saltwater, my friend!" said Mechanic. "Saltwater will certainly water your garden . . . "

Chef finished the sentence totally embarrassed, "And kill it, too!"

Mechanic shook his head.

"I warned you about Foreman, didn't I? Give a fool a job and get foolish results!" He turned to leave.

Chef called out, "Wait a minute. What should I do? I need water!"

Mechanic handed Chef a shovel. "Dig a hole deep enough and you might find water. Good day, Chef!" Then he left.

Chef's mustache shook with anger. "I'll dig a hole all right," he hissed.

"AND WHEN I FIND FOREMAN PIG, I'M GOING TO MAKE SURE HE'S AT THE BOTTOM OF IT!"

PIG DREAMER

Pump loved the Pig Top Circus. He was always the first in line for a ticket and watched every performance, day or night. He couldn't get enough of it!

He loved the smell of the grease paint, the sawdust, and the spotlights! But more than anything, Pump wanted to be a star in the Pig Top and to be the greatest circus pig ever!

Pump was usually a very shy pig, but one night he gathered up enough courage to ask the Ringmaster if he could join the circus.

"Maybe I could be an acropig or a trapeze hog? What about a fire-breather?"

The Ringmaster looked at Pump doubtfully. "We don't take on just anyone. We need pigs with skill and flair." He studied Pump steadily. "What have you got to offer?" he asked.

Pump shrank back and felt stupid. He didn't have an answer.

The circus pig felt a little sorry for Pump and added, "Look, come back when you think you have something to show me. Then I might think about it. Maybe one day, okay?"

That night, Pump hardly slept.

"The Ringmaster was right. I have nothing to offer," he thought.

As he closed his eyes, he could only think of the circus.

The next day, Pump awoke tired and fed up.

"Perhaps today," he thought, "I should think about what I could do as an act."

Besides being shy, Pump was also very clumsy. He either broke things or tripped everywhere he went. This made Pump even less confident about himself.

Despite this, Pump worked for Mechanic Pig.

He moved engines and passed tools to Mechanic (which he sometimes dropped!), but this wasn't Pump's dream job at all! He got bored easily at work and daydreamed a lot.

One time, Mechanic caught him distracted and gave him a lecture. He said,

"YOU'RE WASTING YOUR TIME, DREAMER!"

"You're lucky I gave you a job, because you're useless! Get your head out of the clouds and maybe you can become successful like me," he said sharply.

This made Pump feel even worse, so on his break he went to the park to clear his head.

He liked to sit in a rubber tire that swung from a tree there. It was one of his favorite spots. All he could think about was the Ringmaster's words: "What have you got to offer?" And the Mechanic's "Useless!"

The more he thought, the higher he swung.

Lost in thought, Pump didn't realize he was going so high.

The tire swung full circle and went out of control.

The tire spun faster and faster, and soon Pump couldn't stop. He screamed,

"HEEELP!"

Then the rope snapped! The tire bounced down the street with Pump stuck inside it. He tried to jump out but couldn't.

"Someone help me, please!" he yelled.

Pump bounced over a roof and headed straight for town.

City pigs jumped out of his way to avoid getting squashed by the tire.

They shouted,

"LOOK OUT!"
"WATCH IT!"

Today of all days, the Ringmaster had gone to the cake shop to buy buns. As he was leaving, Pump whizzed by and almost knocked his top hat off. The Ringmaster exclaimed,

"CRIKEY!"

He watched in amazement as Pump first demolished a flower shop and then plowed through the cake shop window with a giant crash, sending sticky buns everywhere.

The Ringmaster saw onlookers burst into laughter as an embarrassed Pump emerged from the ruins with cake decorations and fillings splattered across his face.

He was the laughingstock of the city as he sulked and headed back to work. One pig shouted out,

"HEY PUMP, ARE YOU OKAY? YOU LOOK A LITTLE PASTRY! SORRY, I MEANT PASTY! HA, HA, HA!"

When Pump arrived at work, Mechanic asked, "What have you been doing? Look at the state of you."

"I'll get cleaned up," said Pump bashfully.

"There's no time. I have an urgent job for you. I've fixed the Ringmaster's circus buggy and I need you to deliver it to the circus right now."

"But I look like the stupidest pig ever," complained Pump.

"You'll have to go as you are," warned Mechanic sternly,

"AND PLEASE DON'T MESS THIS UP!"

Pump's heart sank as he started the little engine.

PLIPPETY-POP!

PLIPPETY-POP!

It puffed gray smoke as he set off toward the circus.

Pump headed through town but soon started daydreaming again. All he could think about was what he could do as a circus act.

He wasn't concentrating and drove recklessly through the streets.

City pigs jumped out of his way to avoid getting squashed by the buggy. They shouted,

"CAREFUL!"

"ROAD HOG!"

"FOOL!"

Suddenly, Pump took a corner too fast and bumped into a large tree root. The buggy nearly tipped on its side but balanced on two wheels and carried on down the road. This snapped Pump out of his daydream. He panicked and tried to wrestle it back onto four wheels.

He narrowly missed crashing into the Ringmaster, who was on his way out of town with his sticky buns.

"I say!" said the Ringmaster, "that's my buggy!"

Pump, not quite knowing what to say, shouted, "Morning!" The Ringmaster could only watch him shoot by.

Then Pump hit a big pothole that threw him out of his seat. There was a loud crunch, and a back wheel fell off. Still, the buggy carried on.

"Three wheels! Three wheels!" Pump squealed.

Nuts and bolts flew off with every bump.

He braked hard, but nothing happened, and like a rocket, down the hill he went.

The Ringmaster gave chase.

Pump seemed to hit every tree and boulder in his path, which made even more pieces fly off the buggy.

Ahead was a deep canyon with a bridge. Pump knew he was going to miss that bridge.

"YEEEAARGH!"

The Ringmaster watched and held his breath as Pump hurtled toward the drop.

Halfway down, Pump smashed into two boulders. Two more wheels broke off, and the buggy itself stopped dead in its tracks.

Pump sighed with relief. "Phew!" Then with sheer joy he shouted,

"OH YEAH! WEE-HOO!"

The Ringmaster hollered, "Hey! Are you all right?"

Pump was mortified that he'd seen the whole thing.

The Ringmaster called again. "I said, are you okay?"

Pump shouted back, pretending to be brave, "Yes . . . of course I am!"

Unfortunately, in doing this he dislodged himself and the buggy, which started back down the ridge toward the cliff's edge.

"Oh no! One wheel! One wheel!" he screamed.

Then without warning, Pump hit a large, smooth rock on the edge of the drop and catapulted off the edge.

"YEEAA!"

Pump made a safe landing on the other side of the gorge.

"Fantastic," said the Ringmaster in disbelief.

Pump and the single-wheeled, mangled wreck went faster than ever.

"Not good, not good!" he shrieked as he jiggled down a hard, rocky road and shattered most of his teeth.

TWANG!

FLUP!

R-R-RIP!

The road took him straight to the circus, where suddenly he flew off the end of a ramp he didn't see coming, did a triple somersault, and tore through the circus tent.

One of the circus acts was a high diver who used a gigantic water-filled wooden barrel. Today the barrel was on its side, empty and being checked for leaks.

Pump landed inside it and whizzed around in a blur. He spun around the wall three times then hurled out like a comet toward the circus ring.

As he shot past the fire-breathing boar in the middle of his rehearsal, he was barbequed like a pork sausage.

CRACKLE!

Pump left behind him a trail of smoke and flames and plunged into a container of safety custard used for clumsy acropigs.

All went quiet. The Ringmaster pulled up in his cart. He had seen the whole thing, just like everyone else.

Pump's head popped out of the wobbly yellow goop. He was too embarrassed to face his heroes.

Everyone just stared at him.

"I broke your buggy," he said and immediately felt stupid for saying it.

"Yup," replied the Ringmaster, "you sure did!"

Pump tried to explain, "I've wrecked it. I'm really sorry." Poor Pump just wanted to hide in a hole.

There was a long silence.

Then the Ringmaster burst into laughter, followed by the rest of the circus.

The laughter grew louder and louder.

"Pump, you must be the worst driver in the world, but the funniest pig I've ever seen!"

"Funny?" asked Pump.

"Why yes, I think you have found your natural talent, young pig!"

"Have I?" asked Pump cluelessly.

"Pump, you will make a fantastic clown!" the Ringmaster exclaimed. Pump looked confused.

"Pump, we don't have a clown. Come and work at the Pig Top!"

Pump stared.

"So what do you think?" asked the Ringmaster.

A big, gap-toothed smile spread across Pump's face as he realized he'd just fallen into a job—literally!

AT LAST, HIS DREAM HAD COME TRUE!

From that day on, Pump was known as the funniest circus act ever, and he hardly had to try. He just had to be his clumsy self!

THE END!

INSIGHT KIDS

PO Box 3088
San Rafael, CA 94912
www.insighteditions.com

Find us on Facebook: www.facebook.com/InsightEditions
Follow us on Twitter: @insighteditions

Written by Les Spink
Illustrated by David Baldeon
Colors by David Garcia
Graphic Design & Layout by Mikko Hiltunen

Library of Congress Cataloging-in-Publication Data available.

ISBN: 978-1-60887-377-7

 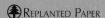 REPLANTED PAPER

Insight Editions, in association with Roots of Peace, will plant two trees for each tree
used in the manufacturing of this book. Roots of Peace is an internationally renowned
humanitarian organization dedicated to eradicating land mines worldwide and
converting war-torn lands into productive farms and wildlife habitats. Roots of Peace
will plant two million fruit and nut trees in Afghanistan and provide farmers there with
the skills and support necessary for sustainable land use.

Manufactured in China by Insight Editions

10 9 8 7 6 5 4 3 2 1